For Ruth

Hank sends you these
poems, with thanks
and love...

Ann Mullert

Arias,
Riffs
&
Whispers

Words Written for Voices
by
Ann Medlock

Bareasss Press
Whidbey Island, Washington

Copyright 1978, 1983, 1986, 1995, 1996, 2000, 2003 by Ann Medlock
All rights reserved

Manufactured in the United States of America

Design consultant: Susan Holt of pixelgraphics.com
Typefaces: Goudy and Papyrus

Library of Congress Catalog Card Number 2003092444

International Standard Book Number 0-97411066-0-7

Cover art:
Ena and Betty, Daughters of Mr. and Mrs. Asher Wertheimer 1901
by John Singer Sargent ©Tate, London 2003

The paper in this book meets the guidelines for permanence and durability
of the Committee on Production Guidelines for Book Longevitiy for the
Council on Library Resources.

Poems in this collection have previously not appeared in any journal or
magazine you may think they'd be perfect for.

They are published here by Whidbey Island's

Bareass Press

which is accessible by ferry, by calling 360.579.8457 or by e-mailing
bapress@whidbeyisland.com

The website for Bareass Press is called www.annmedlock.com, to foil cyber
porn seekers, who would be terribly disappointed.

To

Lisel Mueller

whose clear, stunningly beautiful voice lives on my nightstand and travels

in my luggage, reminding me of the power words have when wielded by a

true artist. She sings from the summit of the mountain I'm scaling.

Contents

Dear Reader... 8

The Sisters...

Miss Ena Wertheimer's Fan 13
Witches 14
Sea Sister 16
She Does Not Sing For You 18
Sonoma 20
Melusine's Footprint 21
Luisa 22

Above & Below...

Tonantzin 26
Signals from A Resistant Species 28
A Mandala for Sisyphus 29
Sharbat Gula 30
Mandela 31
Spa 32
Delusional 33
Lost, or Found, in Queens 34
Anima 36
Her Muse 37
Space/Time Non-continuum 38
Nouveau Moscow 39
Michelangelo's Hand 40
Brackets and Tethers 42
Flying Blind 43
Zero Sum Grace & Favor 44
Joseph Campbell's Pockets 45
Clergy 46

Watching Mother Work..

The Sound 50
Gotcha 51
Big Sur 51
Working the Wisteria 52
When Monarchs Die 53
Damage Control 54
Mistery 54
North of Seattle 55

February at Five 55
Evergreen Code of the West 56

Pseudobio...

Dolores 58
The Meanest Man in Horse Creek Valley ... 59
Officer of the Deck 61
Iambic Recollection 63
Talking to the BVM 64
Sweet Peas and V-mails 65
The Way It's Done Here 66
On the Inland Sea 1955 68
Ahfrrikah 70
The Guy from Cap d'Antibes 73
Saigon 1960 74
R&R 76
Two Coffins 1968 78
Manhattan May 80
Park Bench 80
Unicorn 81
Eddie 81
Unsaid on Star Island 82
David 83
Ode To Sir John of Cambridge 84
Understanding Cortez 85
Heresy 87
Destination Final 89
Solveig 90
Figure and Ground 91
Tracking Homo Domesticus 92
Sauna 92
Familiarity 93
Erasure 94
Even Song 95
Envy 95
The Brick Hat 96
Frame 97
Hurry Up Please, It's Time 98
Arms 99

Arias, Riffs & Whispers

Dear Reader...

There's a minuscule circle of people I've been calling Dear Readers for a while now, giving them these pieces to read in little handmade books: *As If These Were the Endtimes, End Times Two,* and *Millennium Red.* The enCouragement of those Dear Readers has coaxed this chicken-hearted writer into taking the circle public.

I've been a rather public person for some time, though wearing another hat. "Googling" my name turns up the Giraffe Heroes Project, the nonprofit I founded out of my concern for the health of the body politic. Under its rubric, I've done articles, profiles, a website, OpEds, radio commentaries—all of them about heroic behavior and the need for more people to stick their necks out for the common good. I do understand the need to be brave and in some parts of life, I actually am.

Before a giraffe ate my life, I was a freelance writer and editor in New York, Chicago, Washington DC, Saigon, Kobe and Leopoldville. Particularly memorable moments: being in the press gallery on Capitol Hill as the civil rights voting act passed; jetting to Paris to write a speech for the Aga Khan.

In a word, I've been busy. As well as chicken. The nonfiction work is solid ground that I walk confidently, knowing it has redeeming social value. Here, I'm stepping straight off a cliff, and the action may have no societal merit at all, but here goes.

For several years I was an active board member of Hedgebrook, the world's best retreat for women writers. It was a joy to help give women the time, the moral support, and the physical coddling to find their voices and get what they had to say on paper. But doing that for other women did beg the question: when would I take my own turn?

One nudge forward came when the *Washington Post* published an article some months after the September 11 attacks, headlined "Beauty is Back." The writer saw us turning toward the solace of the music, painting and architecture of earlier times, away from the edgy, ego-driven dissonance of modernism. It struck me that perhaps things might be circling around to where I had came to rest, despite being out-of-step with the culture. I'm transfixed and restored by the grace and beauty of other times. The pen I sign letters with has real ink in it, the forks I eat from are deeply worn sterling, the house I live in a timeless one. Sargent's century-old paintings give me goose bumps, and I couldn't write dissonance if I tried. If beauty is truly back, I can stop feeling I got here a century late. If beauty is back, those of us who treasure words we can understand, words that engage our emotions rather than challenge our intellects, all us unfashionables, may not be so out of it after all.

Poetry, as defined by many literary journals, is so intensely cerebral, sometimes so deliberately inaccessible, that it's left many of us not-necessarily-dumb readers thinking profoundly, "Huh?" I finish a page, read it again, and still wonder what the writer was getting at. What I find myself writing is so unlike that, I decided, as you saw on this cover, not to call this work poetry. If we just say these are words written for voices, maybe we get closer to the humanity of this form of writing, to the impact of words coming from the physical mouths of human beings, into the sound chambers of fellow creatures' ears, moving from there along the nerve endings and veins, to lodge deep in their bones.

I always hear voices when I write these pieces, not the schizophrenic kind I hasten to add, but performers, diving into the words, chanting, whispering, singing, roaring, laughing, pounding out a beat. There's something tribal about it, a handing along of experiences, warnings, revelations, blessings.

As a longtime feminist, I'm particularly aware of how many sisters in the tribe have moved me along the way. Susan Gray, Chandra Holsten, Heather Ogilvy, Cynthia Repplier, Jo Rothenberg, Anne Marie Santoro, Mary Schoonmaker and Susan Scott have been right there, blocking me when I try to withdraw, insisting that this work matters. There is no birth-sister in my world; the girl who was to come before me "drowned," the term then for a still birth. She left a space that's been filled by chosen sisters, and they've done a splendid job of it.

Special thanks to Anne Devore for the elegantly professional boot-in-the-butt; to Sherwood Ross and Peter Tavernise, for the pats on the back; to T George Harris for the verb, "to bareass;" to Goody Cable, Andrew Carroll and Gloria Steinem, my back-cover blurb writers, for astonishing me; and to John Graham, whose presence in my life is so integral and so cherished, you'll find him on many of these pages.

—A.M.

Should this book find its way into the hands of My Editor,
the one who thinks this *is* poetry, let's talk. I just don't have time to search for you.

The Sisters...

Arias, Riffs & Whispers

Miss Ena Wertheimer's Fan

Ena's burgundy velvet, her sister's white satin
welcome the touch. You can see the pulse in
their young round arms, shoulders, necks,
feel the press of Betty's wrist at Ena's waist.

One, two, twenty certain strokes and the fan
is in Ena's hand, ready to conceal a foolish whisper.
"Mr. Sargent is so handsome.
Do you think he'll stay for dinner?"

The speed in those strokes,
the rush to leave, to get on with real work.
"Things that matter await my hand—
soldiers, Bedouins,
brooks, hillsides in Spain,
authors, Presidents,
Christs,   gourds.
Here are your daughters, Asher,
where is my bank draft and my cab?"

Witches

Far down the stone passageway, a key turns,
a heavy door is pried open and shoved shut
as the passageway funnels to our acute ears
a woman's scream
reeling high over the deep imprecations of our jailors.

It is time. They are coming.
The uncertainty ceases now,
the not knowing when they will end this.
We will leave this constant blackness
that has kept from us the passage of the days and nights,
the movements of the clouds, of the stars and of our moon.
We will walk into the light and time will begin again,
for a little while.

Another scraping of keys, another cell opened,
its contents reamed into the corridor, moaning in terror.

We will leave behind these walls
that have bruised and chilled us, sister,
walls that have kept from us
the grace and beauty of the world,
walls that have left us only the sounds
of our own whispers, the feel
of unyielding stone, rough straw, our own parched skins,
and of vermin coming to live in these once beautiful rags.
We will no longer sip the stench-filled air of this place
but drink deeply the intoxicating scents
of our Mother's beating sea and blooming herbs.

She will warm us with Her sun,
send Her breezes to our faces and through our hair,
She will send wrens soaring over the courtyard,
She will flutter the leaves of the poplars that rim the square.
I will see your face again, sister,
not with hands that smooth away your tears
but with eyes that welcome the sight of your goodness.
Perhaps   perhaps   there will also be
beloved faces in the crowd.

A closer door, a voice we once heard singing,
now raised in rage.
It is answered with the sound of a blow
and a fierce bellow that roars up out of fear
far deeper than that which stops our breathing
as a key enters the lock that has kept us here.

We will not cower in this darkness,
hoping they will not see us.
We will not stay in this hell that they have made.
We will go now, good sister,
into the joy of the Mother's glory
which will reign triumphant all around us
as these fear-filled demons burn us out of these bodies,
converting us at last, to light.

Sea Sister

She hears the ship splinter and crack.
It shudders and is pulled through the seatop
out of the known world
down into some other, terrifying realm
where air cannot fill its sails,
where weight and darkness rule.

The spar she holds with bleeding fingers
is ripped away by the fierce water,
purposefully, as if it has better uses for it
than saving her life.
The sea shoves, presses, twists her about,
bruising her, hating her.

Her long cotton dress,
the thick petticoats beneath,
all heavy with seawater,
pull her downward.
She fights to stay in air,
seeing the rescuer,
willing him to see her.

He has found her sister,
has hauled the girl up
out of the hateful sea
into his small wood boat.

Look this way.
Here I am, too, in the sea.
Sister, tell him to look for me.

She rises with a swell,
joyful to be carried up
despite her leadenness,
to be borne closer to the white sky.
But the high ridge becomes a valley,
and she is taken down
where they surely will not see her.

She rises again to see
their backs are turned.

Look here, look for me.

But she sees no searching eyes,
only the blue arm of the fisherman
around her sister's back,
holding her safe in a wooly brown blanket.

Drained of strength, she loses the air
and is pulled through and down.
No longer able to fight the water,
still she wills the man
to know where she is,
to fetch her back
up into the light, the air.

Look down here.
Let loose the child in your arms.
Come down here.
Pull me into your small wood boat.

But he does not come.

Eyes tightly closed against
the silent world she has entered
she can still see their backs,
their safe, floating, breathing backs.

Damn them.

She opens her eyes
to what surrounds her now
and sees a garden of seavines
reaching up to entwine her.
She flails at them, furious,
gasping for air, she is filled by the water
and sees nothing more.

She is back. She is here. She is angry still.

To Donne who yearned to heare,

Yeats who pursued,

And Eliot who was right...

She Does Not Sing For You

Glittering, curving, unknown
    to sky, land and flame,
    she pauses in her confident progress
    through her realm and circles you curiously.
The water between you
    heats as she turns, her hair haloes
    around her lovely calm face,
    dancing against your cheek as
    she looks into your eyes
    and comes to some conclusion.
A slight turning of a sleek shoulder,
    an indolent muscling of her tail and
    she is gone.
Your yearning is unimpressive,
    your predicament immaterial.
    She is seeking more than you offer.
    And you saw no way to enter her
    mysterious body, have no way to remain
    in her world, although the undersea

beguiles, and you long to plunge into
her warm center.
Loins, lungs, heart shout counter commands—
Leave. Follow her.
Go back where you came from, trudge heavily
on the mundane ground, fill your chest
with fumes and dust, still yearning,
still questioning, but knowing now
she soars and spirals here, jubilant,
garlanded in flowers of the tealgreen sea,
holding no memory of you.
Or, you may die, here, in the backwash
of her indifference.
She did not give you her secrets,
did not breathe for you, open to you,
smooth away your pain,
envelop you in beauty,
call you by your name.

Vain, cold, soulless killer of good men—
the bitch will pay.

Sonoma

In the Valley of the Moon, the mountains are women.
They lie serenely silent, protecting us with their gentle warmth.
Lion mothers with golden hips, breasts, shoulders, calves
all coated with golden grass whose waves chart the wind's caress.
Live oak trees line their folds with green-black softness.

Two human daughters of earth,
we walk an ancient trail through the valley,
remarking upon the manzanita,
inhaling a cool breeze that smells of the sea,
starting at a scurry in the brush.
City women, unaccustomed to striking fear
in small, wild creatures,
we laugh at ourselves and hurry on.

Abruptly, we come upon a high meadow,
a place we know in a moment is unlike any other.
Here there is no trail and, without a word,
we wade separate courses into the waist high grass.

The full moon rises behind a leonine shoulder,
a pearl medallion transmitting some message from the lavender sky,
the light goes silver and carries in stillness.
No breeze moves the earth's fur, no clouds sail, no creatures amble.
We barely dare to breathe the deep, sweet scent of earth that enfolds us.
We are of the stillness, and the only movement is in the heavens
as the lioness releases the moon
to float into the now violet sky, towards the Pleiades.

A doe lifts her head above the grass and considers me,
holding her ground, deciding something of great import to her, to me.

The air moves again, but it is no longer of the sea.
It is warm, warm as sighs, moving our hair, caressing our faces and arms.
It is of earth now, from the mother hills, benediction and embrace,
a gift spreading over the valley in widening waves, blessing the grass,
the doe, the moon, and all who have ever walked here.
Now we are of this Valley of the Moon, welcomed and nurtured
by the powers who rule here, who have ruled here always
and will remain forever, embedded in these lion woman hills.

Melusine's Footprint

There were promises, sincerely made
in the grip of love,
children borne and cherished,
but a promise is a promise
and he has broken his,
has spied upon her private
meeting with her oceanic self,
kept what he's seen secret until
in fury he has hurled it forth.
His hold on her is broken
and she is gone, as she promised,
returned to fin and tail,
drawn home to her own,
one human footprint left for him
at their window over the sea.
One oval, four small circles over
a moon shaped arch,
wrench his heart from his body
into the lunar driven waters.

Luisa

I was looking uptown, the day so clear I could almost see
my building there, in the Bronx, way up the A line, and the school.
I was saying a prayer that the first day of second grade
was going well for Eduardo, when I saw the plane.

The sky was always full of planes,
but this one, this one was all wrong,
not flying where the others did.
Help them, *Madre de Dios,*
something is terribly wrong.

It came at us, low and straight, on purpose.
I saw the belly as it hit above us. I saw it
and all the windows shattered.

I could not see Luisa but I could hear her
screaming, at the desk next to mine
in the huge space where the data clerks worked,
on the floor below the brokers.

I clear my eyes and shout at her
Luisa take my hand!
She cannot hear or see me.
I use my sweater to wipe away the blood
on both our faces. I think she is hurt very badly.
I push open a stairway door, pulling her behind me.

People are coming down from above,
burned people, sobbing, stumbling.
Step down, Luisa, step down.

So much smoke it's hard to see,
but I feel the metal rail with my hand
and Luisa's hand with the other,
wet, soft, cold, it does not hold on,
like Eduardo when he is very very tired.

We go down and down,
with people pressing all around us.
She falls, I pull her up.
Step down, Luisa, step down.
But she can barely move.

I move her through a door into a quiet place,
empty and beautiful, letters on the mahogany desks,
coffee in a china cup.
She wants to rest in the soft blue chairs
but we must not stay.
We are making dark marks
on the thick cream carpet.
I think she is hurt very badly.

Step down, Luisa, step down.
Firemen push past us, climbing up with tanks of air.
They look at us and shout *Keep going.*
There are medics in the lobby.
Keep going down. Hurry.

She says she can't go on,
she must sit on the stairs.
But there are too many people,
they will step on you, they will fall on you.

Luisa wants to push through another door, to find soft chairs,
to rest and then go back up to our desks,
back to our work, back to our lives.
She does not understand that she may be hurt very badly.
Stand up, Luisa, we must go down.

The stairway shudders and I am falling.
There is nothing to hold,
to keep us where we are.
Everything is falling.
There is nothing to hold that is not falling.

I am the falling, the roar, the cloud,
I am the force of the earth as it halts the fall,
I am the fires that begin to burn, there, there and there.
I am the Mother mourning for her sons and daughters.

In my massive silence,
only the twittering sounds of the firemen's jackets,
telling their brothers where they've fallen.
They come, hundreds, looking for them, for us, in the ruins,
thinking they have not found us, but they have.

Flesh into smoke, smoke into flesh,
our bodies powder their faces, line their lungs,
the seekers of the missing, breathing as they dig,
looking in vain where we'll never be found.

Luisa thinks she's back at her desk, there in the air.
Not understanding what has happened
she reads the pages, keyboards the numbers,
frets about her children and if she'll get a raise.
She is surrounded, above, below, and all around,
by hundreds more who also do not understand.

Stop now, Luisa. Step away from your work
and into Holy Mother's arms.
What held you there is in the rescuers' bodies now
and in their prayers of grief.
Step away, good daughter, you are free now to step away.

Above & Below...

Tonantzin

All right that's enough.
Over four centuries of this nonsense
is quite *quite* enough.
The black Madonna. Her picture on
Cuauhtlatohuc's robe.
Roses in December. *Castilian* roses.
Mary, Queen of the Americas. *Mary.*

Listen and listen closely.
My name is Tonantzin, mother of all the Aztecs.
That was and is my holy place, the high ground
where I was worshiped for a thousand years,
the ritual place where Moctezuma
received Cortez into our ancient world,
before the betrayals began.

I gave you life, I will see you into earth
when you die and I am not black, I am golden.
I am not some wispy Florentine girl
posing in pretty robes for a Raphael to paint.
I have bones, substance, the presence of command,
and I wear the clothes of my people, my arms bare
in the heat, crowblack hair gleaming in the sun.

Note to performers:

The Nuahtl pronunciations are:

Toe-nahn-TZEEN, Koh-WOUT-la-toe-HOOK, Mau-cot-lah-eh-CAOW-teen. No is no.
Good luck.

I do not look down daintily but straight
into your wavering eyes, seeing you
for all you are and are not. Unlike this
Mary girl, I am not easy to live with.

I do stand on the moon, I do radiate light—
even fools get some things right.
And I take some satisfaction in the spread
of this frail usurper, this Madonna of Guadalupe,
as her sweet image appears around the world.
They could not have taken away my people
without her but in truth, I have the people still, and more.

You know, you *know*, that this Mary thing
stands for me, however palely, that she is me,
Tonantzin, that she is Isis, Astarte, Freya and Sekhmet,
all of us who have been banned from your world
by the priesthoods of the timid.
You put this Mary on your dashboards
and on your refrigerators because your fears
allow us only insipid form.
Still we reign in your lives, creating it all, behind this silly girl.
Mauhcatlayecoantin! No *Mauhcatlayecoantin.*
Fools!   My fools.

Signals from A Resistant Species

Solstice night *stille nacht,*
moonless, cloudless, mistless, windless,
every star attending and mirrored in the marsh.
Beauty above us, beauty below us,
beauty before and behind us,
looking low, looking high, looking over,
losing bearings, losing balance,
we stop ourselves from falling up
as we approach the massive flames.
Handmade light and builtup heat push
against the blinding dark and killing cold
that are this night.
We are witness but not subject,
admiring what is here, what is now,
while fighting it torch and log.
We send sparks swirling up—and down—
to dance in the black sky and in the black water.
Hey God are you getting all this—
the silver pinpoints of your stars,
the golden pinpoints of our fire?

A Mandala for Sisyphus

The brilliant lines and
shapes take form,
grain by bright grain
as orange and burgundy
robes border the table.
Golden hands infinitely
precise and certain
put down tiny trails
the colors of cardinals,
jays and cockatoos.
The last grain placed,
they step back, crown
themselves and begin to
sing strange harmonies,
chords made not in concert
but from each singer's
body. The sound and
the form draw us in
to disappear into beauty,
into the perfection
of what fills our eyes and
ears, into joy that humans
can do such things.

The sound stops.
One bald monk steps to
the mandala and swiftly
calmly claws perfection
into chaos and it is gone,
dumped into a jar and
marched to the sea by a
parade of laughing monks
who will do this all again
tomorrow and tomorrow
creating, enchanting
then consigning to rivers,
lakes, seas and ponds,
the ruined remains of
their stunning skill and faith.
One must imagine Sisyphus happy.

Sharbat Gula*

Seaglass eyes in the desert
green fear glaring forth
above a defiant mouth.

Russian bombs have fallen
in range of those young eyes,
have orphaned her, sent her

to walk through snow to the
camp where the foreign man
asked "May I take your picture?"

Take your picture.
Take it to windows, kiosks,
mail boxes, fridge doors,
to Brooklyn Kobe Lagos London,

a fierce and nameless girl,
infinitely multiplied on paper,
locking eyes with the world.

Your concern cannot erase
what she has seen, restore
what she has lost, but it's
kind of you to care, to
wonder if she lived.

Her daughters clasped close
to her purple burqa, she looks
out from a page again. The soft
skin is lined now around those
eyes you know. They ward
your bombs away from her
children. Those eyes fear you,
from her world of sand.

*Sharbat Gula is the real name of "The Afghan Girl," the long-anonymous child in the *National Geographic*'s most famous cover photo.

Mandela

In his eighth decade he stands here free,
emerged from the caged years, from
the unintended monastery where reckless
fire became the molten gold radiating now

in his gaze, his voice, in the hand
that holds Graciella's as he turns to
leave the room, still guarded by
blond Afrikaaners, surrounding

him, glaring menace at the eager
crowd, pressing against us to
clear his way to wherever he wishes
to be. A searing flash from a

contraband camera and the white
phalanx springs closer to him,
arms raised—to protect.
"No flash! No flash!"
they shout. "It hurts his eyes."

They are gone.
Mandela, his love,
his white guards,
and any certainty
we may have had
that time brings
only loss.

Photo taken by the author, without flash

31

Spa

Tecate's women cross the grounds,
smooth warm clay in motion,
sculptures down from their pedestals,
moving to chambers booked solid for the week.

Tecate's women will soothe away
the wrinkles in pale fuzzy skin,
unclench muscles wound tight by
infighting on the fortieth floor,
by alimony battles and Junior's
third involuntary drug rehab.

Tecate's women cannot be found in
elevators, conference rooms and airplanes.
They walk the ground that they are of,
giving present form to the genes
of a thousand years, right here, in this place.
These are the bold bones, the black eyes
that welcomed Spain, not far from where
you are standing.

> Give us your tired, your rich, your
> yuppie gringas yearning to
> stop hyperventilating,
> trying for some reason to be
> bonier. We do not share such concerns.
> The curve of the earth is rightly echoed
> in a hip, a breast, a calf.
> But we will soothe you, heal you,
> send you back north,
> feed our black-eyed children with your tips—
> you are welcome here, pobrecitas.
>
> De nada, señora, de nada.
> You will come again next year?

Delusional

He hears a pachink when the child falls.
Another for the grandfather. Louder
yet for the clean shot at the pumps.
His head rings like a neon arcade
triumphing the points of his kills
as real blood warm pools into
living schoolyard grass onto
the gas station macadam to
swirl with the rainbowed
spills. It's virtual, man.
A game with losers
and a winner.

The trainer of mounted police tells his men
to see rabbits when they must control
an undesirable crowd. When the cop
rides over the hippie hunched small
over her fallen child's fragility he
does not see a mother and son
he would give his life for at
any other intersection—
he is clearing a street
of rabbits.

That woman there in the hooch door
may be hiding a grenade behind
the infant in her arms. The
possibility conveys
permission to fire
at The Enemy.

Add just two to the body count to
the millions beyond reckoning
beyond any prospect of reason
of acceptance of rationality.
Our sanity dangles from
our own delusions.

Lost, or Found, in Queens

An urgent search
a plane to catch
a Ford to dump
we're out of time
the map's no help.
Semis blare
neon blinks
tailpipes belch
tempers burst
words burn
planes ascend with purposeful, on-time roars
but the missing rental car lot refuses to appear.

We turn a new corner, perhaps the right one,
and face a wonder in all the grime and roar.

At the edge of the cracked sidewalk,
between a metal warehouse for tires
and a glaring McDonald's—
a low wood fence and an arch of roses,
real ones, live, red, blooming, and behind them,
a small house, pale blue paint immaculate,
windows sheered in white over planter boxes spilling out
elegant evidence of a gardener's art.

Anomaly, incongruity, impossibility
but there it stands, no mirage.
By all the rules they should be gone,
the gardener and the curtain maker,
gone in despair to public housing,
the noise, the thieves, the stench, too much to bear,
their perfect pale blue house
bulldozed in seconds for a Taco Bell.

But they have not gone.
They have sewn and painted and dug and planted,
cooked and talked and called the kids.
They have gone on, here,
here where bleating traffic
traps two astonished travelers outside a gallant arch,
witnessing one improbable patch of life and grace
refusing to succumb.

Anima

Porgy heads north behind a goat—
he *will* find out where she has gone
his glimmering girl, his junky Bess.
He can live without walking, always has.
But he cannot go on without Her.

Priests wear dresses over their trousers,
Marists even to the Pope. Hers are their
favorite prayers, her image is on the chains
around their necks. But they are not
worshiping a Goddess they tell us,
merely the mother of the one true God.

The writer stares at the paper, moaning for
his muse. Nothing will appear until She does,
whispering in his ear, not minding that it
will be his name on the book, the poem, the story,
with no mention of how he heard the words.

Soldiers gut-shot on battlefields cry out
for their mothers when GI Joe mutates
from plastic to agony. Make it right, mama.
Make the pain stop, give him back to life.
She cannot.
But they know where to turn with their prayers.

Her Muse

The man bear barricades her way home,
slamming up barn doors
he has flamed with orange and gold oils.
The known avenue to safety is gone.

All around her, his massive canvases of men's backs.
They are painted power, muscled walls
beautifully bemedaled with the golden signets of bees.
Ensnared by his art, she is disappearing into his being.

She spins to panoramic windows,
seeking buildings, lights—some sign she knows.
But gleaming-racked, stately elk are there,
moving ponderously across craggy peaks.

All in silence, his mate, the teacher,
herds the beasts toward the man bear.
Cursing, he backs away from his captive

who begins to breathe, move, speak.
Filled once more with her own dreams,
she reaches out to him and says,
Stay. Work beside me.

Space/Time Non-continuum

This cannot be Dunkirk.
Dunkirk is where Stukas strafe
the beach and water as Tommies
wade out to the trawlors and yawls
that have come cross channel to take them home.
There cannot be changing cabañas
and soft drink vendors at Dunkirk.

Arbeit macht frei is still above the gate
as we are urged onward not by SS thugs
or *sondercommandos*—by tour guides.
We are free to turn and stroll away
back to room service and down comforters
and to our tickets home. In this time
a trip to this place does not end in an oven.

Reach through the decades. Pull them into now.
Here Reggie, have a beach towel and a *citron pressé*.
Samuel, Rachel, walk away from this place where
you did not die. Live. Have great-grandchildren.

> *The Management apologizes for the misunderstanding.*
> *You were not supposed to be in this water*
> *on this ground, in those most regrettable moments.*
> *We hope there are no hard feelings and look forward*
> *to doing business with you at your earliest convenience.*

Nouveau Moscow

You grew up seeing the pictures—
Fierce men in fur hats, standing on Lenin's tomb,
the Kremlin's fortress wall behind them
and before them, marching troops and missiles
poised to kill you.
Now stand here, a guest of the new regime,
both feet dead center of Red Square, August 2000.
In front of you, Lenin's tomb, with no one on its roof,
no one trooping by, no one waiting to revere the mummy.
Turn now, moving your eyes past St. Basil's
preposterous domes, coming to rest
your back to Lenin, facing the doors of GUM,
the vast arcade once filled with long damp lines
of gray-clad, gray-skinned people
waiting grimly for potatoes, for cabbage,
for poorly sewn clothes that would soon shred—
dreary goods for patient comrades in silent queues.
Look there, see? Over the entranceway—
an icon of Jesus now stares across the Square,
straight at lonely Lenin.
And through the new plate-glass doors—
a Calvin Klein display.
Lenin, Jesus and Calvin Klein.
Welcome to millennium Moscow.

Michelangelo's Hand

Giancarlo steadies himself with one hand
against the fabled ceiling
as with the other he gently wipes away
the veil of centuries,
incense and wax, sneezes and coughs,
all that has turned
the Master's exuberant palette into elegant gloom.

They have been here for months, reversing time,
while the world debates the dangers, the proprieties.
Are they destroying the irreplaceable?
Making mundane the ineffable?
Could the Master really have been so brash?

Giancarlo smiles as his careful cloth reveals
a swath of purple so vivid it stings his eyes.
Bravo, Maestro. Bellissimo. Ben' fatto.
He moves himself along to mark the next small quadrant
he will assay, bracing himself against a browned leg.

With a gasp and the speed of a burn,
he pulls the steadying hand to his face

looking at it in confusion.
Slowly, he moves it back to where
it fits perfectly into the imprint of an earlier hand
pressed into the plaster when it was soft and white
awaiting the exact colors of sunlit flesh.

He stood here, just where Giancarlo stands
his hands raised as are Giancarlo's
his right laying in his figures, quickly,
before the matrix sets, his left testing the surface
where he would manifest a muscled thigh
when the stucco's texture is not too soft, not too dry.

Giancarlo shouts to the others and one by one
they mount the scaffold to place fingers, thumb, palm
into the revelation, here all these hundreds of years,
unseen by the generations looking up in awe.

Each touches, pulls back, and touches again,
feeling life charge from the Master's hand to his.
Joyful communion, gift of grace, a blessing and a wink.
Grazie, Maestro. Grazie, per tutto.

Brackets and Tethers

She brackets his world,
her love, her daily work
the uprights that wall away the void
holding in what good remains
keeping him fed clothed cosseted
safe within the bounds she sets
as old echoes drown out current voices
familiar doors and furnishings move themselves
to confusing, bruising positions
memory invades present time to make
her pale, white-rimmed face not that of his
freckled, red-haired wife but of some frightening stranger.
Muscles, organs chart their own aberrant courses
tipping him over, pinning him to chairs, sending
knives to wake him in the night to the sound
of his own weeping, and of her voice saying
"There, there. There, there."
Terror re-forms as fury, leaps over the loving walls
she holds around him, to make it all her doing.

He is both *lieb* and *arbeit*
her career: his needs, the tethers
that bind her tautly to his side
as she reels under the same bodily betrayals
adding to them his repelling rage.

Dreaming of something else, she is held in place
by knowing he would tumble into the darkness
if the tethers went slack in his shuddering hands
if the brackets she must hold firmly around him, fell away.

Flying Blind

White mass passes to starboard
grazing our hull,
but there is no rending of steel
and we do not sink from the sky.

The mass is benign, insubstantial,
water not frozen but inflated,
a jovial mountain of fluff.

Confident, tested, we sail straight
through another, dead ahead,
and are hurled about the cabin
by its fierce internal forces.

Now hear this—
The pummeling was for impertinence,
for condescending assumptions
and criminal innocence.

Know your selves to be guests,
here at our sufferance and subject
to removal, surrounded, outnumbered.
Guard down, you will be judged unworthy
to stand the posts that are your lives.

Alert to every possibility, placing
each foot, each wing just so, you may
be permitted to pass through our territory—
land, water and sky—all of this that is ours—
with only minor scrapes and bruises.

Your attention is required, and respect.
If you choose instead arrogance, not to worry.
Replacements are ever arriving.

Zero Sum Grace & Favor

Your win my loss, the fence around a couple,
a family, a circle of friends, a class of schoolmates,
holds in an allotment of good,
says there is just so much to be had
and the balances must always be calculated,
the dabs of luck, the dollops of joy
meagerly dispensed within each closed encampment.

Don't get too much now—
You keep your mitts off my share.

What if we blew the walls and let it all in,
all the triumphs, all the kudos,
all the foot-stomping, hand-clapping,
good-on-you jubilation?
What if we welcomed it all no matter who it favored?
You'd rejoice with your mate, your bud, your sib,
your chem lab partner,
and expect the same from them
when the bottomless basket of benifices
spilled its blessings into your own grateful hands.

Joseph Campbell's Pockets

What do you know, Joe,
after all that study, all that tracking
of humanity's search for the sacred,
for import, for course coordinates?

A veritable Harpo of revelations
he pulls from a vest pocket "Natural Music"
and tells us that Jeffers got it right:
to be holy is to be strong enough to hear
beauty in the world's storms and rages
without divisions of desire and terror.
A back pants pocket yields a wallet and
a tiny newsprint clipping in which a Honolulu cop has,
on sight, proffered his life to save a stranger.

Unconditionally living in unity,
namaste in action,
meeting always in Rumi's field,
feeling Qi pulsing through us, it, them, that,
no divisions, no judgments, no fear.
All the scholar's learning distilled in a few lines,
plain, clear, and—
enragingly, divisively, terrifyingly—hard.

Have you another nugget, Joe,
perhaps an easier one,
in some other pocket?

Clergy

Rainey steps back into the spotlight,
    bright dots of sweat
    shining on her clear skin.
    She cues the combo
    and moves into the mike.
The set is half done,
    Ellington, Loesser and Kahn
    the elegant fabrics
    she's laced in, around and over.
Now it's a Lazy Afternoon
    and the beetle bugs are zoomin
    and there's not another humin in view.
She soars and dives,
    gravels a high note
    and Janis is here—
Drops like a cut-cabled elevator
    to press a deep, low phrase
    straight into your chest,
    invoking Morgana, Nina and June.

        Incantation,
        Communion,
        Transubstantiation—
Joy rises.
Not pleasure—
Joy.
Rainey's walking on water
Invincible, taking us with her, to the far shore.

The "clergy" here honored are Rainey Lewis, singer; Jon Zahourek, painter;
and Christopher Alexander, architect.

Zahourek spits on God
    aiming his heat
    at commandments and collections
    as if they were religion.
And while he rants
    life riots through him,
    pouring out of his hands,
    exploding onto canvas.
The driving, relentless force of the universe
    roars through one tense, angry Czech
    and he makes miracles of it,
    there, before our eyes.
Cadmium, alizarin, cerulean and umber
    turned by his rapid hands
    into shadows and shoulders, tendrils and thighs.
The forms write and breathe as Zahourek,
    drunk on the beauty of the earth,
    on the warmth of flesh
    and the ecstasy of movement,
    sweeps us with him, into the sacred.

Alexander sculpts a building
    out of air and wisdom,
    waving his hands,
    squinting his eyes
    to see what only he and God can see
    in this clearing on the bluff.
Listening to something
    we cannot hear, he brings into being
    a house so solid, silent and calm,
    so embracing, consoling and inevitable,
    that it draws in and restores
    every open soul that finds its way here.
And many do.

Pilgrims who have heard,
   who've seen a photograph,
   who sense that here there is something
   mysterious, rare, perhaps even inspired.

On a clear blue afternoon
   we sit at a long table in the sun,
   the house embracing this garden
   and all of us who bask here
   amid calendulas and ferns.
Feasting on tabouli and cold birds,
   we talk of poetry and paintings,
   of terraces in Tuscany and homemade wine,
   of our work, our passions, our quests.
We are friends, gathered here
   by the grace that emanates from this holy place.

At Christmas, the clan assembles.
The tree, dressed in familiar ornaments,
   touches the coffered ceiling
   and sends the scent of balsam to mingle
   with fire, roast and cakes.
Thick walls hold out the cold, the wind,
   and every danger of the world we know.
Comets cut across the high windows
   as we are drawn in and held fast, together,
   blessed by the house that Alexander made,
   while listening to God.

Watching Mother Work...

The Sound

We're the Crusader, out of Petersberg,
    bound for whaling grounds.
Creaking, dipping, rolling with the sea's heaves
    till we enter the still, flat Sound
    as guests.
Will they accept our presence, receive us?
We wait, attending their deliberations.

And they come. The first ones afar,
    spouts against the shoreline.
Then a pod, to starboard, in arms' reach.
They slip under us, tenderly, rising aport.

The sound. The sound.
Air drawn in to those enormous lungs,
    sighed out slow and strong,
    translating for every sea being
    from Drake Passage to the Bering Sea,
    giving them light, giving them voice, here,
    where we can listen in.

More come, they stay, and grow familiar.
Awake and dreaming we hear them,
    breathing for their world.

Gotcha

Clouds pretend to be mountains until
    they move, revealing their massive joke.
Petals fall from the cherry unblemished and
    play in the wind, as if they were detritus.
Lizard says he's rock, chortling as
    we pass, missing him completely.
Water laps benignly then reforms as
    tsunami, biting off the beach and
    all the pretty houses.
Mountain stands serene in snow and
    silent, curving symmetry,
    enhancing views and property values,
    until she tires of the charade and
    claims her true volcano soul.

Big Sur

Moon silvers my bed
Far below the ocean breathes
I feel your presence.

The year's longest days
Spent on this blessed ground
Are you sure we can afford this?

Working the Wisteria

Staring at the spring sky from a hammock
under live oaks, next to a dry arroyo,
the rare and precious indolence is affronted
by a loud drone of industry.

Inside the nearby arbor the roar deafens
as hundreds of big black bees busily
rob the lazy limp blooms
of their drunken nectar.

The lavender pendants consent
to gravity and every breeze,
offering no resistance to them,
or to these intense assailants.

Heady scent induces wisterial lassitude
as my hair moves with these breezes
and my weight is held in place
by the same commanding force.

Affront gives way to shared submission,
but I am safe from the dutiful thieves,
bearing no treasure that could distract them
from working the wisteria.

When Monarchs Die

The spirits of *Los Muertos* fly in, millions of them,
as always, right on time for the day of the dead,
knowing their way three thousand miles
home from their annual exile in *El Norte*.

The hated cracker father lives through tubes,
his tormented wife and five grown children
standing by, filled with the the sight of his dying,
unsure of how to feel when the sumbitch lets go.
His legacy acids through their lives, scarring generations.

The venerable gingko drops every leaf
in one quick release, giving way completely,
holding nothing back, knowing it will
return in full at the appointed time,
as it always has.

The reigning stars sink out of sight
and we do not miss them,
knowing they aren't gone,
just circling over other eyes, for now.

> None of this surprises.
> But when word comes
> that the ancestors have died,
> all of them, all at once,
> millions of wings stilled,
> grounded, acres of them
> in delicate airy layers
> up to our pollened calves,
> we freeze in place,
> as they have,
> not wanting to shatter
> their fragile cadavers,
> not knowing what has happened here.

> Stunned, we join their icy stillness.

Mistery

Mist foments mystery
as it huddles in the hollows
hiding from the annihilating sun
which militantly mounts the mountain
burns off our cover, dispelling the spell
to leave us looking at each other, fully revealed.

Damage Control

The deep white pack eases down the steep warm roof,
revealing red metal at the roofline.
The pack curls down, far over the eaves,
cold trumping gravity to hold there, seemingly unsustained,
ending in improbably long tendrils of thin clear ice.

With no notice, no shift of wind or light or sound,
the faint gray sky sends down new snow,
miniature points of crystallized mist
falling fast and straight, toward the hidden ground.

Hour after hour, the patient, unceasing fall repairs the places
where our woodstove made red swaths,
where our boots had marked the hills,
where our shovels cut dark paths.
And everything is white again, as if we weren't here.

North of Seattle

Rain threads race down,
invisible against white sky
slicing clear against green-black cedars.
The mountains have gone, and the islands.
Whiteness has taken away the world.
Herein this zoomed-in universe,
a fire dances orange and gold.
Wet skin warms to pink, the breath slows,
taking in the blessings of baking bread
and the sweetness of apples.

February at Five

Startling late arrival,
forgotten in long absence,
Sol has sneaked south,
ducked beneath the weight of cloud cover,
darted through small openings
    in the thick black trees
to paint gold shafts down long dull trunks,
to pleat them all light dark light dark,
to prance right through wet foggy glass,
to point warm fingers at
    a yellow chair here,
        three tangerines there,
to prod us with a, "Look, how beautiful."

Evergreen Code of the West

Express shots from earth to God
bold straight trunks, our branches
fragile afterthoughts useful only
for briefly collecting snow which
we may or may not let fall
as you pass among us,
if the wind visits,
if the temperature rises a degree or two,
if the weight begins to annoy.
You want to hang a swing,
build a tree house,
climb one of us for the view?
Do not mistake us for the amiable
eastern oaks you remember so fondly.
We are not here for your amusement
but for our own purposes,
which we are under no obligation to reveal.
Did you call us the-hell-with-you trees?
You seem to imagine your opinion matters.

Pseudobio...

Dolores

What did they know to choose that name?
Did they even know that it meant Sadness?
How did they know to call their sunny angel Sorrow?

"Smile," the portraitist said. "When you don't you seem so terribly sad."
Golden girl, chosen one, so blessed. And so terribly sad.
The answer is not in the room, nor perhaps in the life.
It is a mystery beyond the reach of those arms
    no matter how much she might yearn to know
    the source of such grief.
Another life perhaps. Back there where the girl in the long cotton dress
    was pulled from the sea
    while her sister watched, and drowned.

She veers away from knowing the reason for the grieving
    as she veers from the terrifying magnitude of her joy.
How is such jubilation contained, understood, fully felt, let free?
A great windmilling stride—jubilant, flinging strides
    that threaten to take flight—
    a painting of traveling clouds, mounted high and blinding white—
    arms spread wide before a thousand instruments and voices,
    every movement evoking the sound of God.

Instead
she veers off to read, to watch, to tidy,
action preventing presence,
the comfortable discomfort of putting dreams aside
    to be practical
    to get the job done
measuring out this life in tasks completed
not in paintings, not in poems, novels, stories
where she must face and give form to her grieving, and to her joy.

The Meanest Man in Horse Creek Valley

"If I was that ugly, I'd at least stay home with it."
The child laughs, thinking it's a joke, but he is glaring
at the women passing the porch where the old man
and his Yankee granddaughter rock.
"The Levelheads, I call em," he says loudly,
so the women have to hear. "Look at em.
Heads don't go up and down when they walk."
They look the same to her as the other mill women,
gaunt, withered, pale, but their gliding walk
seems to her beautiful.

Walking toward the company store to buy Moonpies,
one spotted hand holds a cane, the other hers.
"Mind you don't fall. That curb is high."
The cane raises up, comes sharply down
on the shoulder of a black man who jumps into the street.
Eating the sweets on the bank of Horse Creek
the old man deigns to explain. "Nigras don't belong
on the sidewalk when a white man's passing."
He pumps the well handle and she drinks icy
artesian water from the hanging tin cup.
When the cross burns on Cemetery Hill,
he brings her into the sandy yard to see.
She thinks it is a church thing.

There's a photo in the album of this man, young.
You can see the old man coming in the raised chin
in the sneer of disdain. Beside him is a beautiful girl
who is not the grandmother she knows. This is her
father's mother, dead after delivering a daughter,
the daughter taken by the Moonpie rocker
to his childless brother's door, never to nod or smile
as he passed her, growing up in this tiny town
where everyone knew who she really was.

59

She was erased from his life, as was her sister
when she ran from the shell-shocked husband
who was beating her, driven to the train by a gardener.
"She run off with a nigra," the lintheads say
and her grandfather held as how he'd had just one child
and one treasured grandchild, blue-eyed and fair,
a small person who begins to understand
that he is dangerous, Moonpies, and love, notwithstanding.

Officer of the Deck

The sailor stands, arms behind him,
at the stern of the heaving, bucking launch.
He does not move at all.
The child clings to the mahogany bench
as they lurch across the wake
of a destroyer heading out of the harbor
to the sea, to the war.

Her dad will show her how to do that,
absorbing all the boat's motion in the knees.
"See? Like the gyroscope I gave you."
And she'll have sea legs all her life.

The launch comes alongside the battleship.
It looms and snorts, a loud gray machine
sitting solid as a mountain in the water
as the launch bobs beside it.
Sailors move her mother with courtly hands
onto a platform jutting off the ship's side.
High heels click up the steel steps,
hurrying to meet her father,
somewhere up there, on the metal mountain.

The child is lifted as if she weighed nothing
and deposited on the platform
where she freezes, staring at her shoes.
It's too far even to look up, but she does.
And he is smiling down from the sky
drawing her up to where he waits.

In the ward room, officer of the deck,
he sits at the head of the long white table
all gold braid and beautiful manners
as small men in stiff white jackets
serve vegetables carved into tiny creatures.

The ship's whistles, hums and clanks
are muffled by the Mozart
from her father's phonograph.
This is his world, the place where he goes
when they lose him, months, years at a time.

She will try to remember
when he goes missing from her world again,
when the movies show the ships exploding,
the men in the water, screaming
the sea burning around them.
She will hold her father safe here,
in the ward room, all shiny gold,
listening to Mozart, and eating radish mice.

Iambic Recollection

Vanilla scooped onto a doughnut warm
beneath a cozy coat of chocolate fudge
and Boogie Woogie playing from the juke—

It almost seems that fog and death don't fill
the world beyond the steaming windows here.
The Dairy is a place for kids not war
this chilly fall of nineteen forty four.

Along gray streets that dip from here to school
blue stars in windows saying, He's away,
and golden ones that say, Now he's been killed.

Her duties call to her, much stronger than
the juke, not sweet, not warm, not safe but loud.

She must go now and find some fat, some tin.
She must confess, pray long, stay free from sin,
entreat the saints, but most of all, the Lord.

She must sell Bonds and flare some wicks aboard
the Church's rafts of ruby-crusted lights,
not linger here, absorbing like a child
the Dairy's sweet, melodic warmth and peace
if she's to guarantee the star that hangs
in one small window close to here, in San
Francisco's cloaking mists, will hold its hue,
a clear, ungilded, reassuring blue.

Talking to the BVM

Elastic in her veil squeezes her head, the tulle scratches,
    stockings crawl foreignly over her spindly legs.
She hopes that Sister Eulalia will click the cricket soon
    so she can stand and the garter buttons will
    stop digging the backs of her bony thighs.
She looks up at Our Lady smiling down and asks,
    How do women wear these things?
Growing up just may be a terrible idea.
It's not their Father Ryan on the altar,
    it's the bishop himself so there is no telling
    what comes next but soon, soon, she needs to know
    whether to follow the clicker to the communion rail
    or to stay seated here, alone, on the buttons,
    while her catechism classmates get confirmed,
    a public humiliation to her mother
    in front of all the neighbors she has brought
    to watch her daughter's debut as a grownup Catholic.
But if she goes up there with the class,
    she's also going to hell, unless of course
    she can convince the Blessed Virgin Mary
    to talk God out of it.
They should have had confessions this morning.
Yesterday was just too long ago.
She's had a day's worth of sinful thoughts since then.
But there's a war on, you know.
Zeroes could be leaving their carrier
    just over the Pacific horizon
    even as she waits here, in this pew,
    talking to the Virgin.
A direct hit on the church next time
    she steps out of the confessional,
    shiny clean, ready for heaven—
    she doubts seriously there is any other way
    she'll ever make it, no matter how well
    the BVM presents her case.

Sweet Peas and V-mails

Everyday she writes another one,
the flimsy little sheet that folds
into itself to make an envelope.
What can she find to say when
she just wrote to him yesterday?
She writes the address that doesn't
mean anything, doesn't say where he is
ComDesWesPacFor FPO SF Calif.
then puts one sweetpea on the paper
and folds it into an envelope. She grows
the sweet peas, under the window,
at the edge of the victory garden.
Everything grows here, all year,
so there's always a sweetpea for the V-mail.
The girl wonders if they still smell sweet
when they get to ComDesWesPacFor.

The Way It's Done Here

You can't look like that and be smart.
Here always to be attractive
is to be also dim-witted and gregarious.
The bright must be homely and decently reticent
accepting the solitude they've earned.
There is no place in our system for anomalies.
If you insist on honor-rolling we will go blind
and shun you as needs must be done
in this kingdom of the cheerfully average.

She tries to brake her synapses
leave assignments in her locker
answer no teacher's queries
yet she corks up to the light
of disdain unable to sustain
the dumdum masquerade.

They choose her for student council
when she wants to be cheerleader
prom chair when she'd rather be queen
and she does not attend.
Brains don't have dates.

College is for sons.
How thoughtless to imagine she
might go before her little brother
a decade later when he will
party his way to a first-semester
flunkout after she's earned a *magna*
working three jobs to pay the bursar.

A single mother in the Foreign Service?
It's just not done.
Never mind that there are amahs and nannies
abroad and not here. Never mind that your
record is stellar, your accent divine.
We have our ways of doing things
and they do not include diplomats in skirts.

Oh yes there are many opportunities for you in:
(fill in the fascinating field of work).
And you type how many words a minute?

She dreams of a planet, a continent, a nation, a state,
hell she'll settle for a small island or OK—
one household—where *she* can say
This is the way it's done here.
She promises to be benevolent.

On the Inland Sea 1955

A balcony over a beach on the Inland Sea,
artful night waters sometimes painting
hulls and wakes with eerie irridescence,
sometimes rearing back to hurl
typhoon-black waves over the roof.

Instant conspicuousness,
all the wrong colors
in a world of gleaming
black hair and eyes.
Instant illiteracy,
left with only mimed
communication,
dependent on the kindness
of a defeated enemy.

"Our men are dead,"
the explanation by the
thirty-year-old for
why she is picking
up after us instead of
the children she will
never have.

"Please describe your country,"
my students ask, eager
to know about our schools,
our families, about how our
cities work and what we eat
for dinner. There is some
secret of superiority to be found
for why the so long triumphant
have been vanquished.
It cannot be luck—the best win.
They always have.

Earth, man, heaven, the order of flowers,
each stem handled with sensuous respect.
A tapered brush dipped in handmade
ink and moved swiftly across soft paper.
A tunnel made of scarlet maples,
overhead, underfoot.
In the opposite season,
pale blossoms float and swirl around us.
In summer, a soft sail to Awaji, steaming baths,
crisp robes and magical puppeteers.
In winter, toes warm under heated futons
in a lodge of paper ringed by snow drifts,
one exquisite scroll on a bare cloth wall.

We await some match here
for the Japs in the films,
for the Nips in the posters,
some account-due hurled
at us for their terrible losses.
But there are no dark waves.
Only curiosity, courtesy,
and the gentle making of art.

Ahfrrikah

A tree buds, blooms, leafs, molts, buds
in a single week. Say it right—
Ahfrrikah.

Afternoon sky leaps from blue to black,
converting air to down-falling river.
Stops. Goes blue again and steams the ground.
All in minutes.
Ahfrrikah.

Something pointed, acid green,
breaks ground outside the window
and moves upward as we watch,
a coiled tongue, reaching fast
to lick the sun, straight above,
over Ahfrrikah.

Hyacinths mat the river, making islands
we could walk across to Brazzaville,
if the crocodiles did not like to idle there,
black eyes staring up from beneath
the carpet of foreign blue flowers
that stop the river's flow,
invaders who do not belong
in Ahfrrikah.

Priests on Vespas sputter along the streets
their robes and beards flying. Their order
does not require them to dress up like Jesus.
But the heathens they were sent to convert
know how a white holy man should look.
Their semi-Christians will tell you
Paul was here, with images of Christ.
The ancestors carved crucifixes
you can carbon-date to that time
if you don't believe them.
They want to know why we killed our God.
There is more than you know
to Ahfrrikah.

On a high bluff, overlooking the rapids,
a procession of long, lithe bronzes of African bearers
in loin cloths. Their perfect bodies taut with power,
they haul weapons and supplies for the head of the column,
squat Stanley, pot belly pushing out his khakis,
his pudgy hand raised to shade blue eyes
discovering their river. As if no one were here
in Ahfrrikah.

In the *Cité*, a totally white being walks among his brown kin,
a shiver of ice in the sweating heat,
form and texture, Bantu, color   none.
We, the peach-tinted, marvel that he's been allowed to live,
not smothered as evil, as villagers do an unwanted twin,
in Ahfrrikah.

In the *Cité*, the High Life plays and our foreign bodies
nod in time, as our hosts become the music,
moving liquidly within the pulsing laughter of the sound.
Politely, they do not point at their wooden guests
in Ahfrrikah.

A rumor moves through the *Cité*, gathers force.
Do not let your sons go to Louvain to study.
Les Belges tell you they will return, as doctors,
but they are lying. Here is how they return to us.
And the tin is passed from hand to horrified hand.
The one that offers corned beef with a label
of a laughing young man
of Ahfrrikah.

Blacks from America, Returnees, they think,
stare at facial scarring, at filed teeth,
at fishermen in piroques casting nets,
at calabashes moving smoothly on proud heads,
at round brown bellies that hold future Ahfrrikans
protruding from their mothers' jubilant cotton swathing,
at eyes everywhere that judge these mixed-blood visitors
in beribboned straw hats and pressed khaki slacks

to be as foreign as Swedes. This is not Harlem. This
is Ahfrrikah.

Down the long slope of
the hillside, whole villages
pour towards the house.
The vice consul at
the door says "Hurry. Grab
the kids. One suitcase. There's
no time." In the
walled compound of
the consulate, Marines at
the gates, frightened
faces stare out
at the swelling river of
chanting, pulsing bodies
growing larger getting louder,
damming up against the eagled
walls. In the one suitcase,
five neckties and
a bottle of scotch.
Washington is sending
a plane to Brazzaville. Our one
chance a surprise break for
the vedette. A chain of
bodies, men the
larger beads
between the
children and
the women.
"Don't let go of your sister's hand or mine,
no matter what happens."

We are leaving
Ahfrrikah.

The Guy from Cap d'Antibes

The hips try to
lead the body
to saunter
to insinuate
but the belly wins
being ever so much
further forward
overhanging
the minuscule
red bikini.
An astonishing
expanse of
fur coats the
abdominal pillow
spreads up down
perhaps to the soles
of the espadrilled feet
seeming everywhere
except his shining skull.
Shoulders
swaggering
seductively
with every
languid stride
he makes his
unclothed but coated
way along the beach
certain of every eye
smiling confidently
waiting for the women
young, delectable
who will surely be
swept into his
irresistible wake,
following this
homme fatal
to his awaiting bed,
"Not far away, Cherie,
in La Malmaison."

Saigon 1960

There's a dead tiger on the sidewalk
in front of our neighborhood bar
and at the table next to the enormous carcass,
a French hunter cursing the missing client
who commissioned the kill.
We are not in Kansas.

The beached-up Legionnaire
who owns the joint brings unbidden
deaux Gabon, the cognac-and-sodas
that are his *specialité*, dry, cooling, perfect.
His Lao wife and exquisite children
wipe tables, carry trays, fetch Gauloises.
Fragile Vietnamese women float by,
the breezes lifting the panels
of their gossamer *ao dais*, watched by the guys
from Life, CBS and the New York Times,
drinking *Trente-trois* from sweating bottles,
their legs sprawling too casually
from the rattan chairs, all wearing the
safari shirts correspondents seem
compelled to don when they leave
their desks for foreign shores. Vespas,
cyclos and bikes hurry "the locals" by.

Last week a grenade was lobbed from such
a Vespa into a café full of American "advisors."
The death rolls are back, but now
they are made of American names.

Last month, when Diem's own
paratroopers attacked his palace,
we assumed festive firecrackers as
Philippe danced into our room singing
"Boom boom, maman, boom boom."
A machine gun emplacement
five doors away was firing at the insurgents.

Behind shuttered windows, under
a playhouse of mattresses, we listened
to rebel-captured radio. Our neighbor,
kind Mr. Dinh, hurried his wife and children
to the greater safety of our batting-walled
cave and gave us ears on the fighting,
translating the urgent voices that filled
our little fort. The paratroopers had a list
of reforms, would not cease fire until
Diem commited to the changes.
Mr. Dinh shouted at the radio
"Don't believe the lying bastard!"
then translated their annoucement
that Diem had agreed to their demands.
The firing stopped and we emerged
to resume our lives. The paratroopers did not.
All over the city "locals" have died,
and nothing has changed.
Mr. Dinh looks away when he sees us now,
having noted, "Your government could
have saved us from this tyrant."

Last year, when we arrived, the briefing officer said,
"If stopped by a Viet Minh patrol outside the city,
for God's sake speak English.
If they think you're French, you're dead."
Now when they pass, as we have seen them,
silent black forms sliding out of the trees,
a lethal panorama moving across our windshield,
we must pretend to be French.

On a high terrace in Cap St. Jaques,
gazing at the glittering South China Sea,
light dances through a trellised arbor
to play on our skins and on the platter of
crimson mangos that fill our lungs with perfume
and our mouths with enchantment.

R&R

Frantic laughter drowns out fire fights
last week next week an hour away by PanAm.
Tinny band nasal Suzie Wong attempting
Jumpin' Jack Flash.   Failing.

Hands slide into side slits in red cheong sams
knock back mai tais and straight shots
pound tables to give the band the beat.
It's a gas gas gas. Don't you get it?
It's a gas gas gas.

"The Incredible Orsinis" take the floor
tall graying man in a satin shirt
arms raised to bring on with a flourish
"Madame Orsini," a wren of a woman
walking uncertainly on a medicine ball,
eyebrows arches of apprehension
smile an entreaty that goes unseen
as the off-duty combatants turn to
the Suzies and the drinks   bored.
Monsieur Orsini juggles three pins
drops two. This is just a drag drag drag.

Madame Orsini may cry at any moment
but toddles on, mate pointing out
her wobbly progress as though she were Pavlova,
retrieving the juggling pins each time
they escape from his incompetent hands.
There *has* to be a story.

Refuseniks, that's it, they have walked to Vladivostok,
stowed away, gotten only this close, so far, to Israel,
where they will once again be   epidemiologists.
No papers, no money, no local credentials,
they humiliate themselves for their supper in a
Hong Kong dive full of stoned Americans
trying to forget that Charlie is waiting
silent, deadly, patient, never breaking
for Rest and Recreation.

"The Pitiful Orsinis" are taking their bows at last.
I stand and applaud, the sound of one fool clapping.
My tablemates shrug, grin, stand, clap, cheer.
It's a good game. I throw wadded American dollars at
"The Puzzled Orsinis." Bills fly from clumsy hands
all around the floor. Young voices yell
You're a gas gas gas!
"The Incredulous Orsinis"—whoever they may be—
embrace, weeping, and exit left,
with air fare to Tel Aviv.

Two Coffins 1968

Just days ago the calloused feet,
unlike the hands, free of tubes,
moved weakly to the echoes
of a schottische playing across time.
Tonight generations circle the open casket,
the lipsticked face letting them know
they are no longer orbiting Gramma.
She has left me a chocolate pot
and a pattern I will not use
for a life of laundry and devotion,
though I will try, and fail, to
duplicate her cauliflower crisps.
"This is what happens to old people"
says her eldest great-grandchild,
my sanguine son, all of nine.
And he is right. A good woman
has left the world, much in years,
descendants, memories.
Leaving the viewing room, a door
opens on another death, the kind
that does not happen to old people.
Winter-coated, a man and woman
arch over a flag-draped closed coffin,
their heads almost touching,
damp grief conjoining over whatever
may be left of a young Marine.

Semper fi say the gladiolas that will,
in hours, die as Gramma has,
in the proper course of things.
There is nothing proper
in these parents' weighted bodies,
nor in the hidden remains of their son's,
bagged home from a jungle
to be buried in the snow
he made forts of, not so long ago,
perhaps when he was nine.
They hold themselves up
by the casket handles,
smooth the stars and stripes,
as if they were his wounds,
or the fevers the mother cooled
when he had the measles, the mumps,
the charlie horses the father rubbed
with liniment after football practice.
Their hands entwine urgently,
as they may have done when
they made this boy, reaching now
for a way to deal with his obliteration.
I steer my son by his mitten,
away from seeing this other death,
the one that can't be accepted,
the one that cracks the heart.

Manhattan May

Benign air replicates our temperatures,
giving us no shivers, requiring no
barrier between our skins and this day.

Long-naked oaks and elms sport a sudden,
tentative green, whispering chorus for
the giddy pink arias of the apples and
the peach trees.

Families long incarcerated by cold burst
jubilantly into the open, leaving behind
stuffy rooms and withered house plants,
silent radiators and intervening doormen.

They scatter, squealing, as one pussy-willow-
gray cloud sends down a sudden benediction.

Park Bench

Curious, greedy, gorgeous,
the pigeons come incautiously close
as they strut and peck. I toss them
bits of one fresh, crisp, Honey Maid
graham cracker. They mill about
spastically, jabbing at sticks, shards,
bottle caps, Salem butts. Nabisco
makes no impression. I expected
a pigeon Wow, a Hey fellas, over
here! But they're just as attentive
to the pop tops and filter tips as
to a prime edible. Noticing that
I've assumed they're all male,
I laugh and keep all the crackers,
for me and my kid.

Unicorn

Seated in his scent
the evolutionary poet radiates
ideas,
hair,
and the odor of carnivore unmuted.

His message is for those alone
who can transcend their ideas
of how a Source should look, and smell.

Johnny Appleseed of the mind, making sure
his seeds are turned away by fertile ground.
Onanist.

Eddie

The door opens and standing
        there is not the remembered
        lover but some friend
        of her father's.
Who has done this to him?
Who has stolen his radiance,
        leaving him now
        white-haired, lined and swollen?
He speaks and the River Shannon
        flows through Brooklyn,
        filled to its lush banks
        with wondrous aromatic spirits.
The culprit leans against
        the doorjam, grinning.

Unsaid on Star Island

Don't go. Don't take away the lights.
I wanted to say—
the words are locked in here.
I have no voice for them.
But I have hand, paper, pen.
And what I wanted to tell you is
my son is asleep in his room,
breathing quietly, singed pink and gold by the sun.
smudged with dirt, worn still
by the speed of his day on Star.

A simple thing, a child asleep.
But another reality is close now too.
An instant changed, a moment turned,
and I would be having to tell you
that he was out there with the Beebe children,
in the sheltering hollow
where their parents put them so long ago.

I knew that could be
when you walked your lanterns around him,
warming the hard glare of the surgery,
floating him in this powerful sea of light.
I let him go then.
He was free to leave on that good tide
or to stay.
This afternoon he asked me how old he had to get
to be a Pelican.

I sit here now in your steady glow,
loving the strength of these thick, plain walls,
smelling the sea, hearing crickets, gulls, wind,
and an old man saying that his mother brought him
to this island when he was a little boy

that she is always here for him.
My son may say such words in this room,
in another century
because he is not out there in the hollow tonight,
not with those eternal children
below the rose brambles
under the sharp stars.

Listen.
I want you to know.
My son is asleep in his room.

David

His hair embraces his head so well,
no matter how I cut these curls
they turn thickly into his temples
and cuddle the handspan of his neck.

On occasion he reveals himself,
as with solemnity in the emergency room,
his belly filling with blood, he informs me
that he doesn't want to upset me
but he thinks he may be dying.
More often, he maintains his schoolboy cover.

As he grows longer, leaner,
he still manages his old trick
of fitting perfectly into my arms.
He smells of sunlight
as the small currents of his breath
pulse gently on my neck.

Ode To Sir John of Cambridge

Now let us sing to praise our God
for all the manly things,
for the laugh that's bass,
for the lofty view,
for the headlong juggernaut moves
for taking up large spaces
and yearning toward new thrills
on the pinnacles of mountains
while we favor soft, gold hills.
Give praise for impulse, shouts and clanging,
and raucous shaggy-dogs,
for crazy dreams and steadfast plans,
for mischief and for puns.

And also for the quiet within,
that listens, learns and feels,
for the spot that knows and cherishes
the dark side of the wheel.
Let's cheer for all that balances
our yin side of the Tao,
for the glory of the daylight
as beautiful as night,
and for its source
that warmly shares
the heavens with the moon.

Praise God in all Her wisdom
for setting us to share,
to meld and grow and celebrate
the wonder of the pair.

Understanding Cortez

Her lover moves across the room
easy, slow, focused,
still damp from the shower,
ambling toward the closet
where his soft clothes hang.
She can feel the corded arms
that frame his long, sculptured body,
as she watches from the pillows, smiling lazily.

He steps into the square of sun that falls
into this quiet room high above the park
and all the light is caught in one place—
a small stroke of gold on his hand,
drawing her eye, catching her breath
with a wonder she can't explain.

The room fills with armies,
fleets and expeditions
setting forth again and again
to find and, if needs be,
steal this ore from wherever it is,
in the rivers or in the depths
of the deeply veined earth.

They told you in school
it was for the wealth, the power,
but she'd never understood why
any metal could be so treasured,
why it was worth the dangers
that they faced, the price that they paid.

Now she knew
they went forth because they wanted
to hold in their hands
the sun's exquisite presence on earth,
and when their hearts were full,
to melt and shape its beauty into forms
that graced and warmed their lovers' bodies,
as did this glowing ring that,
she now remembered,
marked this beloved as her own.

Heresy

On one of the flat states, New York behind us
Seattle ahead, I dial for a sound to keep
me sentient, on the right side of the line
for my shift at the wheel, for the dark straight
miles ahead, before dawn, before Boise
and the ascending mountains.
Static rules the spectrum until the sudden clarity
of a preacher twanging up from the South
on the quiescent night air waves.
The voice says, plain as day, "Helping others is sinful."
I tune away the hissing sibilants
and await an explanation.
"This here life is, and has to always be, a vale of tears.
Happiness," the word a sneer, "is only in heaven
and only for the righteous."

In no more danger of nodding,
I consider the preacherman's theology
as the dash reads 75 and
the lighted billboards
pass too quickly to read.
Misery is the way of things—
now and through eternity for me and thee;
but only until death for the preacherman
and his adherents. To relieve suffering,
a neighbor's, a stranger's, your own,
is to confound the Divine Plan, a sin of pride.

The gospel according to Hobbes, Lillie, Steig
and Reverend Bob.
Life is nasty, brutish and short—
We're rotten to the core, Maude, rotten to the core—
People are no damn good—
Helping others is evil—
Two of them were kidding.

So hire more cops, build more jails, stash more guns.
If you want to be safe in your bed
during your hideous sentence here,
you'll be looking out for Number One,
you'll be watching your back. And you'll be packing.

If you were in this speeding Pontiac, Preacher Bob, you
would not aim for Aldeberon, smiling at the possibilities that await
after we climb up toward the stars, then down the western slope.
Would not relish the snores of a young son
in the back seat, dreaming of new worlds.
Would not thrill as I do that I can touch the face of love
by simply moving this hand to a bristly cheek,
an arm's length away.
Would not rejoice in the power of this engine,
the thrust of this steel room through space and time,
holding within so much that is precious.
Would not delight in a roadside diner that serves up
peanut butter pie.
Would not bless every seeming mishap
that shoved us to this perfect moment.

Ingratitude precludes paradise not someday
but now, here, where the self-blindered, refusing to incarnate,
do time in their own hell, surrounded by unacknowledged grace.
I shall think on them, sad wretches, but not too much,
as we pursue and experience happiness,
helping others up when they stumble,
giving thanks through all the days
for all that we have. Here. Now.

Destination Final

This is all as I said it would be, and more.
A steadfast house, looking across trembling alders and the still Sound
    to the stunning ferocity of the icy mountains.
A steadfast house, filled with the touch of down, wool, silk
    and the crisp pages of books.
A steadfast house, sounding of cellos, guitars,
    and the voices of poets,
      smelling of bread and lemons.
Here there is a high hearth for sitting before the fire.
Here there is lamplight and kindly worn carpets.
Places for silence, for watching the wind, eavesdropping on the rain.
Places for laughter, for talk of the world and of our journeys.

The way here was long.
Continents, oceans, cities, none my place.
But I have found my way home, at last and forever.
Somewhere in this garden—I have not chosen the place,
    this body rendered ash will end.
I am not leaving here.

For all the days before then,
I have brought tools here and seeds,
    sketches, outlines, dreams,
To this high place where no one has lived before.
Here I came, as I said I would.

Grace was with me
And as I planned, as I dreamed,
I did not come alone but with a great love.
Here, with me, is the one who knows who I am
    and, knowing, wants no other.
One as strong as I, as clear and true,
Welcome left to my essential right,
    balancing, countering, realizing,
      so these dreams I have are more than only that.
We are at home. At last and forever, this is home.

Solveig

My replacement has arrived.
I see her—small, fair, eager,
        already beginning to draw, to write stories
        and I know her.

My replacement has arrived.
She knows me too, knows my house is hers.
I paint stars and poppies on the stairs
        to delight her now
        and when she will climb them here without me.

I begin to gather up what I know,
to leave cake crumbs in the forest
        for her to find and follow.
My replacement has arrived.

Figure and Ground

Each pane of the old window
　　framed a different crag of the range.
On the days when she was there to see them
　　she knew he was somewhere on one or another,
　　too far to see or hear, and yet she
　　saw his scarlet parka marking his location
　　sharply against the snow,
　　saw him kicking spiked boot toes into a wall of ice,
　　saw his long legs pistoning him over a crevasse,
　　heard him jangling his gear and tackle, laughing.
The mountains were magnificent, jagged,
　　torn from the earth too recently for softness—
　　an ungloved hand passed over them would be cut,
　　no matter how gentle its intent.
The Sound lay broad and still
　　below the upthrust range, distancing its dangers
　　from where she stood, her brushes
　　smoothly revealing on gessoed paper
　　the perfection of water without menace,
　　tempering, balancing the peaks where he went,
　　an ice axe in each fist.
An eagle swept across the panes, taut wings wide,
　　storming the black-green firs that sentineled the house,
　　landing fast, claws first, on a high branch
　　next to a white-crowned head already there, just visible.
　　　　He walks across the garden, smiling,
　　　　a coiled hose over one bare, tanned shoulder.

Tracking Homo Domesticus

The house glows and roars in the silent forest—
porch light, hall light, kitchen light, telly,
all blazing, every door and drawer wagging open.
Oven on and empty, pans and dishes abandoned,
coagulating, faucets dripping, fans whirring,
a frantic voice shouting plays
from a tiny speaker in an empty room.
The man of the house is At Home.

Sauna

Golden cedar,
steaming stones, gleaming skins, searing air,
the vent a tiny frame for the scene out there—
black pine, white roof, flakes falling fast.
The radio said two feet by nightfall.
I'll roll in it if you will.

Familiarity

A smiling man programming systems, fathering children, playing bass,
  he connects somehow
  to the zygote detected by the Roman rabbit
  celebrated with trattoria ziti and black-tooth wine,
  to the squint-eyed newborn burping colostrum in North West DC
  far from the rioting Congo,
  to the bikinied boy wheeling his friend Tran down Rue Nguyen Than Y,
  playing in the hiatus between the French war and ours.

> Passing behind his chair at the head of his own table
>   his wife and children settling into their places,
>   I hear a nurse's voice. "There! See? Just one more push."
>   She's showing me, in a mirror, the top of a small head,
>   the top of *this* head, that I see as I pass—is graying.

> I will never comprehend time.
>   But I do know this being,
>   no matter what his form,
>   do remember and recognize
>   the loving awe that welcomed him
>   into the world. It radiates from him,
>   palpable, as he moves through his life,
>   in the roles and body of a man.

Erasure

There, where the gulls are circling
I once spread my arms, offering you
Manhattan, the Bronx and Staten
Island too, throwing in Jersey and a
bit of Connecticut. You laughed and
said—Sold. After the City Hall ceremony,
we drank champagne to seal the deal,
back at the top of the world, there
where the morning crew and the
breakfasting brokers were cut off
by the flames, way up there
where they rode the tower down
becoming dust as they descended,
bypassing in an instant the decades
it must rightly take for flesh and bone
to disappear. We try to comprehend,
looking into the blank sky, at the gulls
gliding unimpeded where once there
were steel, concrete, marble, glass,
upholding human joy and work,
the clink of crystal heralding
the plans of people who would
leave that height and go on to
the lives unfolding before them,
here on the now grieving ground.

Even Song

White, pastel-tinted, iridescent,
the mid-June evening teeters between day and night.
We move inside a vast shell of abalone,
sky and water held apart by one low island.

Quiet Night leaves Danny's sax,
floats over the town and the Sound.
We are tipping into darkness
but if Danny plays Oh What A Beautiful Morning

it may all go the other way.
In the precarious balance here,
we hold out our arms, tightrope walkers
ready to ride time in either direction.

Envy

There is something missing
in my brain-body connection
the link that puts the beat into
the muscles, the joints, the blood,
the switch that says "Forget grace,
get down." It must be accepted.
There is nothing more ludicrous
than an Englisher trying
to dance black.

The Brick Hat

How long does it take
reality to reach and register
below the mind, past the grasp,
in the muscles, the organs, in
whatever place it is where
nightmares learn to be dreams?

The brick hat is shed, yet
the crouch persists,
the weight bearing down
on the unheeding body.

The degree is earned,
the villains vanquished,
the work secured,
the children raised,
the love found,
the wandering over,
home base so long established
there in the sheltering forest,
it's time to re-do the roof.

Yet she dreams of straight, dark,
empty streets, hard corridors of
endless locked facades exuding
danger, loss, dread.

She wakes when he tips their bed
to starboard, as he has for decades now.
But when she lets go of the light,
there is no companion, no solace,
only the long empty streets echoing
the fear in one voice calling out
unanswered in the darkness.

Frame

"Gentlemen, set your frames.
This here dance starts simple
and gets tricky real fast.
Your lady cannot do
the necessary turns and
flourishes if you do not
give her frame.
But if you got
steady shoulders,
rock-like arms,
sure footing,
then there she goes,
twirling, double-timing,
knowing she can count on you
for balance. Give way
when she swings out,
when she's off balance—
her spin will take her down.
Then you got one bruised and
limping little lady, don't you know?"

You ask what I need from you
as I rescript my life, ending what
I thought it was and spinning into
what it may really be. No actions,
no words are needed, only frame,
only the pinpoint touch of your
solid presence, only the stillpoint
without which there is no dance,
and we know there is only the dance.

Hurry Up Please, It's Time

After decades of
donkeying,
of moving
solidly,
bearing
whatever
cargo needed
to be moved,
the load
is lighter,
the bearer
weaker, the
hooves placed
far less
surely, the
old balance
not what it
once was,
y'know.
Vision
blurring,
joints
complaining,
on the
familiar trail,
for some
reason—
perhaps it was something carelessly said over dinner—
the small
gray beast
remembers
that it is a
mustang,
a tall proud roan, mane flowing, long legs pawing the wind,
undomesticated descendant of the Conquistadors' steeds.

A case of
mistaken
identity,
simple but
not easily
rectified in
the time and space
available.

Arms

Small soft peach, petting a cat

firm lean freckled, holding a child

veined mottled creped, keyboarding a riff—

What   the   hell?

"Publishing a volume of verse is like dropping a rose petal down the Grand Canyon and waiting for the echo." —Don Marquis

If you'd like to echo your comments up to the publisher, *do*.

Echoes in the form of orders for more copies are particularly welcome.

Individual copies are $11 plus $3 shipping and handling. For additional copies to the same address, the S&H is $2 per copy. If you're a Washington State resident, add 91 cents per copy for the tax collector.

If you'd like to give the book to friends, ask about getting them signed and gift-wrapped.

Order by mail, phone, email or on the website.

Bareass Press

7285 Fiske Road
Clinton WA 98236
360-579-8457
bapress@whidbeyisland.com
www.annmedlock.com

Coming soon from Bareass:
Walking the Mermaid
A novel about New York in the 60's
&
The Book of the House
A nonfiction look at the only house Christopher Alexander
(*A Pattern Language*, *A Timeless Way of Building*, *The Nature of Order*)
has built in the Pacific Northwest.